SUMMY and IZZY
In a TiZZY

Thea Lynn Paul & Julia Turnbull

Based on a true story.
Story and illustrations by
Thea Lynn Paul and Julia Turnbull.
Illustrations created with alcohol ink.
Hand lettered by Thea Lynn Paul.
Technical assistance by Camie Leard.

Summy and Izzy in a Tizzy

tellwell

Tellwell Talent   www.tellwell.ca
ISBN 978-1-77370-126-4 (Hardcover)
978-1-77370-104-2 (Paperback)

To our grandchildren

MY real name is ISABEL.
Most people call me IZZY.
THEY think THAT'S my real name.
BUT it's not.

Some people think my GIGI is gaga. BUT she's not. She just has the crazy giggles. And I mean CRAZY!

My GIGI took me to the PARK
to MEET my friend. SOME people think
her real name is SUMMY. BUT it's NOT.
Her REAL name is SUMMER.

SUMMY is very funny. Some people
think she's funnier than me. BUT she's not.
Summer has a NANA. Some people think
her name is Banana! But it's NOT.

Some people say "IZZY, your hair is FRIZZY."
But it's not.
SOME people say "IZZY is DIZZY."
But I'm not.
My HAIR is curly and BROWN.
I love spinning AROUND.
Sometimes my feet don't even touch the GROUND!

SUMMER'S hair is LONG and yellow.
It dances in the WIND.
When she SPINS, she GRINS!
I wish MY hair was like Summer's.
But it's NOT.

SUMMER runs from the swing to the SLIDE.
What has she SPIED?

Is it a DOG? Or maybe a FROG? It's not.

My **GIGI** brought me a banana for a **SNACK**.
It's in her fanny **PACK**.
Summer's **NANA** brought her **CHEESE**.
BUT first she has to say "**PLEASE**."

WHEN it was TIME for our SNACK
we both did a JUMPING JACK!
Summer said PLEASE and got some CHEESE.
BUT where is my BANANA?

Summer asked her NANA "Have you seen Izzy's BANANA?"
NANA and GIGI both TOOK a LOOK.
They COULDN'T find it. IS there a CROOK?

IS it in the TREE? No, there's a BEE in the TREE.
Is it in the BUSH? Is it under Gigi's TUSH?
No it's NOT!

GIGI is in a PANIC. She is FRANTIC.

SUMMER shares her CHEESE.
She doesn't make me say PLEASE.
WHERE is my banana?
It was HERE! And now it's NOT.

I see a PEEL! I let out a SQUEAL!
Summer is running all over the PARK.
Then she sees something DARK!

WE look with FEAR.
How does a banana DISAPPEAR?

SUMMER sees a black SQUIRREL.
It's gone with a TWIRL.

IN its mouth is something YELLOW.
What a SNEAKY little FELLOW!

We ALMOST catch the speedy SQUIRREL,
his long TAIL in a giant CURL.
GUESS what that squirrel's got?

My BANANA! Let's tell Gigi and NANA.
What a TIZZY! This makes me DIZZY!

Now it's FOUND!
It's on the GROUND! YUCK!

SUMMY and I are STILL hungry.
Our day will NOT be complete,
without something YUMMY to eat!
GIGI says "Let's go for ICE CREAM!"
We're so happy we could SCREAM.

A wonderful **WAY** to end the **DAY.**
SUMMER and I **LOVE** to **PLAY.**

We HOPE that squirrel will STAY
in the TREE and not run FREE!
But he does NOT...

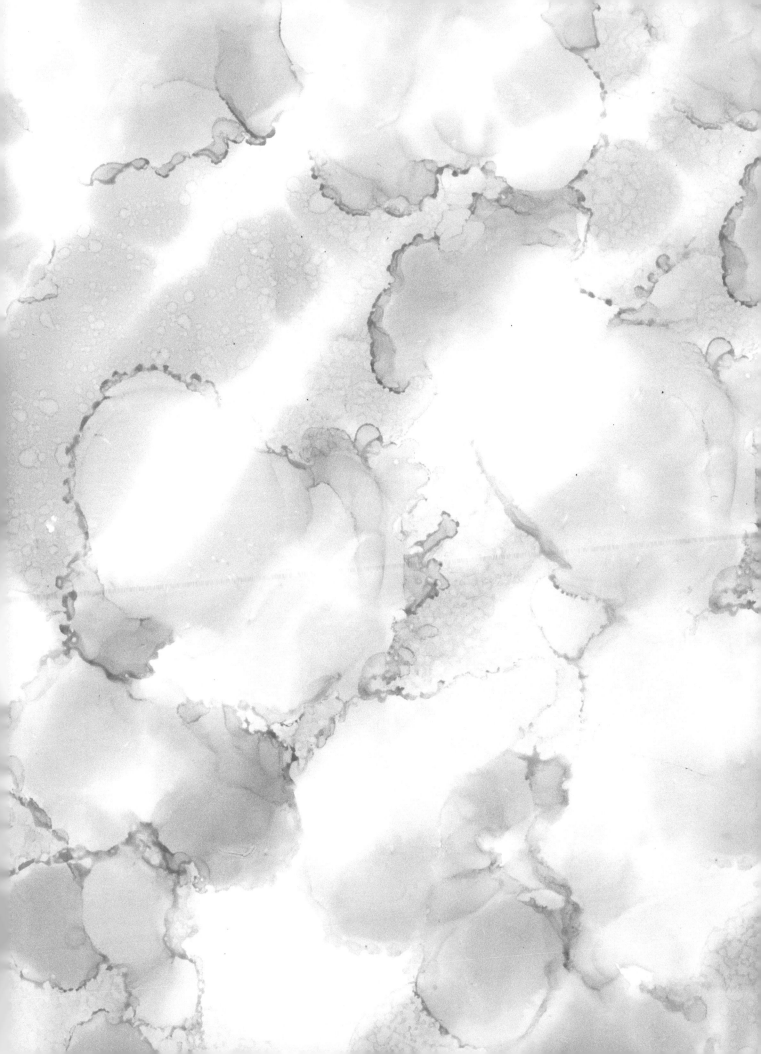

CPSIA information can be obtained
at www.ICGtesting.com
Printed in the USA
LVHW01n1403121217
559442LV00003B/37/P